LEGO DC COMICS SUPER HEROES

JUSTICE LEAGUE™ VS BIZARRO LEAGUE

LOOK FOR LEGO®
DC COMICS SUPER HEROES:
JUSTICE LEAGUE VS. BIZARRO LEAGUE
AVAILABLE NOW ON DVD AND
BLU-RAY FROM WARNER HOME VIDEO

W9-BEO-496

SCRIPT WRITTEN BY MICHAEL JELENIC
ADAPTED BY J. E. BRIGHT

SCHOLASTIC INC.

ISBN 978-1-338-03524-7

10 9 8 7 6 5 4 3 2 1   16 17 18 19 20

Printed in the U.S.A.   40

This edition first printing 2016

Book design by Erin McMahon

CHAPTER 1: SUPERMAN'S TWIN?

IT WAS A SUNNY DAY at the playground in Metropolis. Children laughed as they raced around the equipment, playing on a merry-go-round shaped like an octopus. Their mothers chatted on benches at the edge of the sand, drinking coffee. Behind them in the parking lot was a line of identical SUVs.

The mothers sipped their coffees . . . and gasped as they spotted a blue blur whiz above the city, circling the golden globe atop the Daily Planet Building.

WEEEEε!

"Look!" the first mother shouted. "It's Superman!"

The being swooped down. He looked like a brutish, twisted version of Superman. The mothers screamed as the monstrous creature laughed harshly. Then he crash-landed, giggling, in the sand.

The children shrieked as they saw the scary thing laughing in the playground.

The messy monster became alarmed. He stared at the kids on the merry-go-round as they hollered in the octopus's spinning arms. "Bizarro save tiny people from tentacle creature!" he growled.

The kids screamed again as Bizarro barreled toward the twirling octopus. He yanked it free. Bizarro

SUPERMAN!

grappled with the octopus, and children toppled into the sand. "No like calamari!" he hollered.

The mothers hopped, shrieking in alarm. Kids were crying everywhere.

Bizarro gave the roundabout a solid shake, and two kids flung free, sailing into the sky.

Another blur whooshed down toward the kids.

It was the real Superman!

He caught the children, gathering them safely in his grasp as he hovered. Superman lowered, easing the kids onto the sand.

The mothers sighed with relief as they saw their

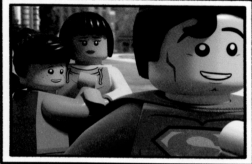

children giggling next to Superman.

"Don't worry," said Superman. "They're just fine."

"Thank you, Superman!" cried his mother. "You saved my child from your crazy brother!"

"Oh no," said Superman, laughing awkwardly. "That's not my brother. It . . . I mean, *he* was created when Lex Luthor hit me with a duplicator ray."

Bizarro smacked the octopus roundabout hard against the blacktop.

"Excuse me," Superman said. He zoomed over. "Bizarro, put that down," he ordered.

"Bizarro put down," said Bizarro. He hurled the

octopus spinner overhead. It wheeled straight up until it vanished. He smiled proudly.

Superman rubbed his forehead. "*Down* means *up*. *Up* means *down*. Why does everything have to be backward with you?"

"Bizarro help Superman!" argued Bizarro, surprised. "Save Metropolis from tentacle creature!"

"Why is it every time you try to help," asked Superman, "Metropolis ends up destroyed? That octopus isn't a creature. It isn't even an octopus. It's not dangerous!" He sighed.

That was when the octopus merry-go-round returned to Earth. It slammed into the SUVs in the parking lot, smashing the vehicles into hundreds of tiny bricks. The SUVs broke into rubble, jumbling their pieces together in a heap.

"Ha-ha-ha," said Bizarro. "Boom!"

"My car!" a mother squealed. "Do you know how long it took me to assemble that? There were, like, so many bricks!"

Another mother pointed her finger at Superman. "Can you take your identical twin somewhere else?"

"Twins! Oh no," Superman said. "He's actually the opposite of me in every way."

Superman flew over to Bizarro.

"Bizarro save Metropolis!" Bizarro cheered.

"Bizarro save home!"

"You sure did," said Superman, shaking his head. Then he looked up into the sky. "You know," he told Bizarro, "I recently discovered a place that needs your help even more than Metropolis."

Bizarro's eyes blazed. "Let's not go!"

Superman nodded. "Follow me," he said, lifting off. "I mean"—he corrected himself—"*don't* follow me."

As Superman flew out of the playground and zoomed high above Metropolis, Bizarro kept close behind.

CHAPTER 2: BIZARRO WORLD

BIZARRO TRAILED SUPERMAN up through Earth's atmosphere, past our solar system, and into the deep void of outer space.

Traveling at super-speed, they soon passed far-out stars into uncharted darkness.

Superman glanced at a handheld navigational computer. He studied the star charts.

"Should be around . . ." he muttered. Then he spotted what he was looking for. "*Ah*, right there."

A planet appeared as Superman and Bizarro flew toward it.

It was an enormous rocky cube floating in space.

Superman dived down, soaring into the cubic planet's atmosphere. Freaky lights flashed in the planet's clouds, shining in kaleidoscopic colors.

Both Bizarro and Superman gasped, startled, when the little computer in Superman's grasp suddenly fizzled and shattered, floating away in broken pieces.

Their entry through the atmosphere became more

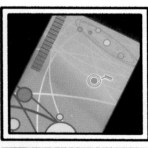

turbulent as they traveled toward the rocky surface below. Superman was badly shaken up. Bizarro giggled at the bouncy descent.

"Where you take Bizarro?"

"Somewhere you can't get into trouble," replied Superman. "This planet's physics are a little backward . . . just like you. It's going to be the perfect home."

Bizarro gazed out on the empty alien landscape. "Home Metropolis," he grunted. "How I save Daily Planet? How I save people here?"

"*Hmm*," said Superman, rubbing his chin. He

scanned the area, noticing the huge golden crystals dotting the desert. "Watch this." He carved crystals with his heat vision. Superman stacked the cut crystals until they resembled a jagged version of the Daily Planet Building with its signature globe. "Just like the one on Earth," he told Bizarro. "What do you think?"

Bizarro stared blankly at the teetering rocks.

With lasers from his eyes, Superman etched a simple smiley face on to a small crystal by the base of the rocky tower. Then he sliced a chunk of the globe

and it slid down toward the smiley crystal below. "Bizarro!" called Superman. "That citizen is in trouble!"

Bizarro rocketed to catch the falling rock before it brained the stone citizen.

"You nothing to worry for, citizen," Bizarro said with a grin. "Bizarro keep safe." He patted the smiling crystal on the back. Its head popped off. "I think I kill him!"

Superman replaced the citizen's stone head. "He'll be just fine," he said. "He just needs to rest at home." His eyes gleamed with an idea. "Can you build him a home, Bizarro?"

Nodding excitedly, Bizarro shouted, "Bizarro build!"

Superman hovered above the planet's severe surface. "I would wish you good luck, Bizarro," he said, "but you'd take it the wrong way."

He took off back toward Earth, leaving Bizarro alone in his new home.

CHAPTER 3: GOING BANANAS

ALL WAS QUIET from Bizarro for a year.

In the meantime, Superman and his powerful friends in the Justice League stayed busy saving Metropolis.

One day the citizens ran screaming down the streets when the monstrous Giganta stomped across the city. With every thudding step she took, cars bounced. Giganta was eight stories tall and wore a leopard skin like a cavewoman.

Giganta shook the Daily Planet Building. "I got news for you!" she thundered. "Print is dead." With a mighty heave, she pushed the entire tower. The building slowly toppled.

Superman swooped in and caught the building. "This skyscraper is heavy." He pushed the building upright.

"Now Clark Kent doesn't have to look for a new job," Superman muttered. Giganta, scowling, raised her fist to punch Superman. A golden lasso circled her wrist.

Wonder Woman yanked her lasso from where she stood atop her Invisible Jet. Giganta fell backward, plopping down with a thud. "Giganta, this is no way for a lady to act," scolded Wonder Woman. "Or dress. Animal prints are *so* last season."

"Leopard spots are the new black," replied Giganta. "And I'm going to make you black and blue!" She swung a vast fist.

Wonder Woman hovered out of the way on her jet. "If you say so!"

Giganta climbed back on her feet, punching at Superman and Wonder Woman as they ducked and fought around her.

Nearby, Gorilla Grodd stood on the ledge of a building. He wore his mind-control helmet. Gorilla Grodd smiled up at the rampaging Giganta.

"The perfect distraction for the perfect plan," he declared.

Grodd pressed a button on his helmet and telepathic energy waves circled out. He was controlling three villains—Deathstroke, the Penguin, and Captain Cold. Each carried crates out of a warehouse.

"The Justice League will never figure out what I'm really up to," hooted Gorilla Grodd.

"Let me take a shot at it," said Batman. He leaped between the gorilla and the villains. "You're using your

mind-control helmet to turn Giganta, the Penguin, Deathstroke, and Captain Cold into your henchmen. So while Giganta wreaks havoc on Metropolis you get your real prize."

"Pretty good guess," Grodd snarled. He reached up to press a button on his helmet.

Before he could touch it, a pair of rocket-powered metal hands snatched the helmet off the big gorilla's head. The hands carried the helmet back to their owner, Cyborg.

"Booyah!" Cyborg cheered. "Batman knew you'd try that. So he had me snatch your hypno-helmet." He crushed it in his fist. "He's just so smart."

The Penguin squawked as his brain cleared.

BOOYAH!

THAT'S COLD, MAN.

"Grodd had us under mind control."

Batman hurled another Batarang, which sliced the lid off a crate.

Dozens of bananas tumbled into the street.

"Nobody makes a monkey out of me," Deathstroke seethed. "Let's get out of here!"

While the villains scurried away, Grodd reached into another crate and pulled out a scary-looking weapon. He shot laser beams at Batman and Cyborg.

Batman flipped away from the deadly beams.

Gorilla Grodd opened the third crate, and put on the jet pack inside. He blasted into the sky.

Batman strapped on his own rocket-powered backpack. "Stay put, rookie!" he ordered Cyborg. He took off after Grodd, past where Giganta was squeezing Wonder Woman's Invisible Jet and Superman in her enormous fists.

The newest Green Lantern, Guy Gardner, arrived in a big green bubble floating over a nearby park.

AW, I WISH I HAD A JET PACK.

"Let me show you how a real hero does it!" he announced. He shined his power ring, creating a gigantic glowing copy of himself, which he could pilot from inside its head.

Wonder Woman rolled her eyes. "Wow, look, Superman," she said. "Guy Gardner finally made something as big as his ego."

Guy leaped at Giganta, but she was ready for him. "Say hello to the agony of defeat!" she shouted. Giganta kicked Green Lantern, connecting solidly

with her gargantuan foot.

Green Lantern tumbled backward and slammed upside down against a building. His giant creation fizzled, and he fell down and landed hard on his head. "Ow," he said.

At least he had distracted Giganta enough for Wonder Woman and Superman to gain the advantage in their battle with her.

Green Lantern and Superman buzzed around Giganta's head, and when she swung her fists at them, she tripped over the golden wire and fell over.

"Wrapping things up here," radioed Wonder Woman from her jet as she wrapped her lasso around Giganta's feet.

Using his power ring, Green Lantern created handcuffs big enough to hold her enormous wrists.

With Giganta under control, Superman contacted Batman. "How's it going with that big gorilla?" he asked. "Need any help?"

In their jet-pack chase, Batman whooshed after Gorilla Grodd, tossing Batarangs. "I don't need any help from you," Batman replied rudely.

Gorilla Grodd plunged through a pack of Boy Scouts, tumbling them into the air.

With lightning-fast reflexes, Batman hurled a dozen manacles, chaining the Boy Scouts together. He caught the whole matrix of scouts before they could fall. Then he took a shortcut, heading off Gorilla Grodd with the connected pack of Boy Scouts.

Gorilla Grodd got tangled in the scout chain. All the little boys clung to the gorilla, pummeling him

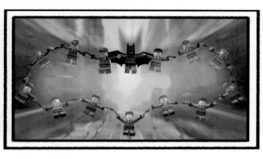

with their little fists.

Batman lowered the ball of Boy Scouts to the sand in the park, with Grodd unmoving in the middle. The scouts all cheered, and Batman pinned merit badges on their uniforms.

"Great takedown," Superman complimented Batman as he landed beside him. "But maybe next time, instead of using children to stop super-villains, call on your friends."

Batman narrowed his eyes and got into Superman's face. "I keep my friends close," he growled, "and my enemies closer."

"I hope not much closer than this," Superman joked. Then he realized how serious Batman was. "You're not implying that—"

Interrupting Superman, Cyborg leaped over and

started singing and dancing in victory, delighting the Boy Scouts.

"We caught Gorilla Groddy," Cyborg chanted, "and now we're going to party. Villains going to prison 'cause the Justice League is winning! Booyah!"

CHAPTER 4: TROUBLE ALERT!

THAT AFTERNOON, the Justice League gathered around a big table in the Hall of Justice, their head-quarters.

Superman hovered at one end of the table. "Great work out there, everyone," he said. "Especially our two new recruits, Cyborg and Guy!"

Cyborg grinned at Batman. "The Man of Steel said I did great!" he cheered. "Fist bump!"

GREAT WORK OUT THERE, EVERYONE.

"I don't fist bump," said Batman.

"When we join forces, no evil can match us," continued Superman. "That's why we formed the Justice League. Together we fight for the liberties of all living creatures. I am proud of your individual accomplishments today . . ."

Batman's mind wandered during Superman's speech. *I joined the League to keep an eye on the most powerful being on Earth,* he thought. *The hearts and minds of man are no mystery to me. But an alien Superman . . .* Hidden from view, Batman pulled out a lead container. *Good thing I have my box of Kryptonite!* He opened it, and inside a chunk of space rock glowed.

Superman dropped to the floor.

Batman shut the box and hid it.

Groaning, Superman stood and glanced around uncertainly. "I'm okay," he grunted. "Not sure what came over me. I must have eaten some bad buffalo wings. Now where was I? *Ah*, yes. A hero sandwich sounds good." Cyborg followed Superman toward

the kitchen.

"Superman sure left in a big hurry," Batman growled suspiciously.

A loud alarm suddenly blared across the room.

Green Lantern, Wonder Woman, and Batman hurried over to the monitors.

"Great Hera!" cried Wonder Woman, studying the screens. "There are reports of Superman attacking LexCorp in Metropolis."

Batman pounded his fist into his glove. "Aha!" he said. "I knew he would snap one day! I tried to warn everyone, but no one would listen—"

Right then, Superman and Cyborg returned to the Great Hall, holding their lunches.

"*Uh*," said Cyborg, "we were just making sand-wiches."

"Don't think I won't check that alibi," muttered Batman.

Superman peered at the monitor. "I have a pretty

good idea of who's behind this," he said nervously. "Why don't I take care of this one solo, guys?"

"I don't think so," replied Batman. "Let's go!"

Superman sighed, but he flew after his teammates as they rushed to the scene of the crime.

CHAPTER 5:
IN THE VILLAIN'S LAIR

THE BATWING and Wonder Woman's Invisible Jet landed outside the LexCorp tower in Metropolis. Superman and Green Lantern touched down near them. Cyborg rode with Batman.

A wide, ragged hole gaped in the wall of the building.

Superman chuckled unconvincingly. "Yeah, really, guys," he said. "I've totally got this."

"And miss all the action?" asked Cyborg. "Uh-uh." He ran toward the hole.

Superman sighed, and flew into the hole ahead of everyone else.

The Justice League followed Superman down

into a gloomy basement laboratory. Various weapons lined the walls in display cases.

"Is this a villain lair?" Cyborg squealed in excitement. "It's my first villain lair!"

By one wall, Batman discovered an open box with a cylinder inside. It was labeled as a Kryptonite bomb, and it included a hologram of plans for destroying Superman. "Lex has been busy plotting our demise," he said, peering at the plans.

Superman flew down beside him.

Batman turned off the hologram.

"Leave it to you to dispose of Lex's evil plans for me," said Superman.

"Yeah, that's what I was doing," said Batman.

"Took you long enough!" Lex Luthor hollered, running into the chamber. "My lab is destroyed!"

"Lex Luthor," Green Lantern sneered. "Do we

really have to help this guy?"

"What's that supposed to mean?" asked Lex sharply.

Superman glared at Lex. "You spend all day creating weapons to destroy us."

"How many times have you framed one of us for a crime," asked Batman, "and then run for president on a platform to stop us?"

Lex smiled. "That reminds me," he said, pulling out a stack of buttons, each printed with the words VOTE FOR LEX. He tossed them onto all the heroes' chests.

Behind them, Bizarro burst onto a high balcony.

"Bizarro!" cried Superman.

Batman tightened his hands to fists. "Another alien!" Cyborg glanced from Superman to Bizarro. "*Whoa*," he said. "Are you twins?"

Superman smacked his forehead. "We are not twins."

Then Superman noticed the weapon Bizarro held. "Great Scott!" he exclaimed. "The LexCorp duplicator ray that created you. You broke in here to steal it? Why?"

Bizarro raised the gun. "Bizarro show you."

"Don't!" shouted Superman.

Bizarro fired the ray. Superman flew out of the way, but the purple beam of energy hit Wonder Woman, Batman, Green Lantern, and Cyborg full blast.

The heroes grunted and groaned as they writhed in pain. They twisted as they were cloned, and collapsed onto the ground.

As Superman sat up, he blinked blearily . . . and

saw five creatures standing nearby.

The first looked like a wrong version of Batman. He turned his mask so it was on straight. "I Batzarro," he introduced himself. "World's Worst Detective."

"I am Greenzarro," said the next one. He whimpered, forming a teddy bear with his power ring, which he cuddled. "I scared."

A junky robot tottered forward. "I Cyzarro—" he said, and then slumped, fizzling. Bizarro flew behind him and turned the windup key in his back.

"I Bizarra," said the female creature. "Pretty, pretty princess."

"Bizarro," ordered Superman, "give me that ray before you do more damage."

"Nothing stop Bizarro!" hollered Bizarro. "Not even Superman!" He focused his freeze vision on the Justice League, encasing them in thick ice.

"Can we go?" whined Greenzarro. "I scared." He used his power ring to make a five-seat bicycle spaceship.

Bizarro noticed a cylinder in a case on the floor.

"*B-O-M-B*," he read. "Boom!" He grabbed it before hopping onto the bicycle spaceship. "Okay," he decided. "Let's stay!"

The rest of the Bizarro League hopped onto the bicycle and it streaked into outer space.

Superman melted the ice block with his heat vision, freeing the Justice League.

"That was weird," said Cyborg.

"How do we know this wasn't always part of your secret alien plan?" asked Batman.

"Because Bizarro can't keep secrets," Superman answered. "He can barely keep his pants up."

"Why make duplicates of us?" wondered Wonder Woman.

"I don't know," replied Superman, "but if one Bizarro can cause this much destruction, think what an entire Bizarro League can do. I know where they've gone: Bizarro World. Let's go!"

As Wonder Woman, Green Lantern, and Cyborg followed Superman out of the lab, Batman hung back.

"So," Batman murmured, "you want us to follow you to some distant planet. Well, I'll play your little game for now, alien."

Then Batman hurried to catch up with his team-mates.

SUPERMAN AND GREEN LANTERN traveled through space on their own power. Wonder Woman flew in her Invisible Jet, and Batman and Cyborg took Batman's spaceship. They reached Bizarro World in the far reaches of the galaxy.

"Merciful Minerva!" cried Wonder Woman. "Bizarro's planet is a cube?"

"I should warn you," said Superman, "things here behave a little—"

"*Um*," Wonder Woman interrupted, "bizarro?"

Batman's spaceship shuddered and shook. Wonder Woman's jet vibrated uncontrollably, too. Both vehicles shattered into tiny bricks.

Cyborg, Batman, and Wonder Woman plummeted toward the surface.

"One rescue rocket coming up," said Green Lantern. He concentrated, but his power ring created a big green

MERCIFUL MINERVA!

chicken instead.

"A chicken," said Batman as they landed. "How degrading."

"I call that use of power ring a clear foul," joked Cyborg. "Get it? Fowl?"

With a scanner, Batman studied a gold crystal. "These rocks are emitting a weird form of radiation."

"We should call it *weirdiation*," said Cyborg. "I like that name!"

Batman shot Cyborg an annoyed glance. "It's this radiation—"

"I do not know what you're talking about," Cyborg said. "Radiation? There are so many kinds."

"Fine," seethed Batman. "It's this *weirdiation* that created the planet and is now interfering with the team's powers and equipment."

"Equipment?" Cyborg peered down at his body, worried. "That's what I'm made of—" His arm fell off.

"Hey," Green Lantern asked Superman, "why

doesn't this place affect you?"

"Well, not much does, I guess," Superman replied.

Batman eyed Superman suspiciously. *So,* he thought, *the Kryptonian lured us to a planet that renders our powers and weapons useless. Well, I have something that will affect him.* Batman patted his secret box of Kryptonite.

Then Batman froze. He hid the box. "*Shh,*" he hissed. "We're being watched." He rolled on the ground stealthily, before popping up beside a

figure on a rocky ridge. "What do you want?" Batman demanded.

Green Lantern flew over. "I think he wants to know why you're talking to a rock."

Batman narrowed his eyes. Now it was obvious that the figure was crudely formed from crystal.

"It's a citizen," explained Superman. "I tried to make this place feel more like home for Bizarro."

From the ridge where they stood, the Justice League now could see a vast city. It looked like

Metropolis, but warped and weird, and filled with crystal citizens. "It's Bizarrotropolis," said Cyborg. "I like making up funny names."

Superman's smile faded when he heard the sounds of a distant battle. "I'm going to investigate."

"Not without me, you're not," said Batman. As Superman flew off, Batman snagged the corner of his cape and hitched a ride.

With a glance back, Superman asked, "Beautiful from up here, isn't it? Oh . . . unless you want us both to fall and become pancakes, I'd keep your lead box full of Kryptonite closed tight . . . *Bruce Wayne*."

"Ha!" cried Batman. "I knew you'd use your X-ray vision on me! But how did you see through my lead-lined mask?"

"I didn't," replied Superman, "but somebody stitched your name onto the elastic band of your underwear."

"Alfred," grumbled Batman.

Superman smiled. "You can trust me with your secret identity. I'm Superman!"

"I don't trust anyone," said Batman. "Also, you're an invulnerable alien whose motives remain mysterious, which means I should especially not

trust you . . . *Clark Kent*."

"Hey," protested Superman, "how did you know my secret identity?"

Batman smiled. "I'm Batman."

Superman slowed for a landing on an outcropping. He and Batman witnessed a surprising scene in the wide valley below.

"That's the source of the sound I heard earlier," said Superman.

An enormous space destroyer floated above the plain. The front of it was shaped like the giant, familiar head of a villain. Behind the destroyer was a hopper filled with golden crystals. Bolts of electricity snaked out of the sides, hoisting more crystals into the ship.

"Darkseid," Superman and Batman said in unison.

CHAPTER 7: TICKLED TO DEATH

THE BIZARRO LEAGUE rushed to the scene, battling to stop the ship from grabbing the rocks.

"Must not save citizens from big head machine!" bellowed Bizarro.

Bizarra pulled rocks back with her lasso, while Greenzarro blocked levitation beams with teddy bears. Batzarro and Cyzarro saved citizens, too.

Inside the destroyer's control room, Darkseid sat on a throne. "Who is stealing my rocks?" he demanded of his henchman Desaad who was working the ship's controls.

"No one, Master Darkseid," Desaad assured his boss. "This is only a minor interference." Desaad

peered at a monitor. "Unleash the drones!"

A horde of drones detached from the destroyer and whizzed toward the Bizarro League.

The drones blasted the Bizarros with lasers, knocking them to the dirt.

"It tickle!" cried Batzarro, giggling.

Up on the outcropping, Superman asked, "They're being tickled?"

"Tickled to death," growled Batman.

Batman and Superman leaped into the fray, smashing drones into scattered bricks.

Inside the ship, Desaad gasped. "Superman?"

"Superman is here?" hollered Darkseid.

"And Batman," Desaad replied. "They have unexpectedly joined forces."

"Crush them," ordered Darkseid.

Down below, Superman and Batman freed the Bizarro League from the tickle attack, and they all fought the drones together.

Superman gasped as he spotted a vast boulder flung from the destroyer.

The boulder smashed down atop the heroes, flattening the area completely.

With the heroes crushed, the ship picked up the remaining crystals in the valley. Then it headed toward the horizon to find more rocks.

When the second the destroyer left, Superman spun upward from a tunnel in the ground. Batman and the Bizarro League climbed out.

"Good thinking," Batman told Superman. "Creating a tunnel saved us all."

Superman grinned. "Was that a compliment?"

Green Lantern carried Wonder Woman and Cyborg into the valley on green chickens.

Batman greeted his teammates. "We're dealing with something big now."

"Darkseid," said Superman.

Wonder Woman and Green Lantern gasped.

"I'm guessing that's a bad thing?" asked Cyborg.

"Oh, he's just the most dangerous force in the universe," replied Green Lantern.

"Is that why you stole the Bizarro ray and created your own league?" Superman asked Bizarro. "To stop Darkseid?"

Bizarro nodded. "Bizarro wanted to protect his citizens from big head machine."

"We can help you," said Superman.

"*Whoa!*" Green Lantern warned. "Easy for you to say, Mr. I've-Still-Got-My-Powers."

"Are you scared, Guy?" Wonder Woman teased.

"Why risk our behinds for meaningless rocks, Princess?" replied Green Lantern.

Bizarro hung his head. "Rocks my only friends

after Superman send me away."

"I sent you here because—" began Superman.

"Because you embarrassed by Bizarro!" Bizarro interrupted. "So you hide him."

"They may just be rocks," Batman broke in, "but I suspect Darkseid wants to harvest their unique properties for a weapon."

"Harnessing their power could render Earth's defenses useless," added Wonder Woman.

"If Darkseid is after these rocks," said Superman, "then he's headed to the greatest concentration of them."

The Justice and Bizarro Leagues rushed to Bizarrotropolis.

"I have a plan," said Batman. He pointed at the pieces of his spaceship and the Invisible Jet. "I'm going to reconstruct the blocks of these vehicles to create a thermodynamic amplifier of the Bizarro ray. When fired at Darkseid's weirdiation supply it will create a new opposite form of matter, and the two will annihilate each other, destroying his ship."

The Bizarros blinked blankly at Batman.

Greenzarro held his head. "All I hear is, 'blah, blah, blah, science, blah, big word.'"

Batzarro raised his hands. "I have better plan," he announced. "First we take nap!"

The Bizarros all cheered that suggestion . . . and conked out.

"I think we should go with Batman's plan," said Wonder Woman.

CHAPTER 8: THE KRYPTONITE BOMB

IN THE CITY, Superman found Bizarro sitting alone with a crystal citizen. "Something bothering you?"

"On Earth I bad hero," Bizarro explained. "On Bizarro World I bad hero. All I want is save the day like Superman." He patted the citizen's shoulder, and its head slid off.

Superman turned the citizen's head over. "The Justice League will save the day, Bizarro. I promise."

After Superman flew off, Bizarro took out Lex Luthor's bomb. "No," he whispered. "Bizarro save day."

At the edge of the city, Darkseid's destroyer collected its crystals.

Superman swooped down to Wonder Woman,

I BAD HERO.

BIZARRO SAVE DAY.

Green Lantern, and Cyborg. "We've got to buy Batman some more time. Let's go!"

In the destroyer, Desaad gasped at the heroes' return. "This is going to make you laugh," he told Darkseid. "Nobody was crushed. Please don't hurt me."

"I will deal with them myself," said Darkseid. He rose on a platform to a hatch on top of the destroyer. He launched a new battalion of drones.

Wonder Woman, Bizarra, Bizarro, Green Lantern, and Greenzarro fought the drones while Superman flew up to face Darkseid.

Bizarra fell into a fighting frenzy, pummeling

drones and tearing them apart.

"By Athena's gray eyes," cheered Wonder Woman, "she is a dog of war!"

"Then why is my guy such a pussycat?" asked Green Lantern. Greenzarro cowered nearby, afraid to challenge the drones.

"Why can't you be more like her?" Green Lantern asked, pointing at Bizarra.

Greenzarro shrugged, hiding behind a citizen.

"You can do it!" shouted Green Lantern. "I believe in you! You're a Lantern."

Then a squadron of drones whizzed at Green Lantern. He raised his ring to zap them but it fizzled. "Still not working," he moaned. The drones buzzed in.

"No!" screamed Greenzarro. He leaped in front of Green Lantern and raised his ring, creating a giant teddy bear around them both.

The drones bounced off the teddy bear, crashed into each other, and exploded.

While working on building a ship, Batman glanced up at the battle. "They better watch for Darkseid's Omega Beams."

"What's an *Omega Beam*?" asked Cyborg.

Darkseid shot luminescent rays from his eyes at Superman.

Superman dodged the beams, but they followed him like heat-seeking missiles. The rays zapped Superman, smashing him into the side of a hill.

"Those are Omega Beams," said Batman.

Superman shook off the painful attack, and zoomed back up to the destroyer to fight Darkseid.

"We'll never let you harness the power of this planet, you space bully!"

"I will," Darkseid swore. "And after Earth falls the entire universe will bow to me!" He tossed Superman off the destroyer.

Superman crash-landed near Batman.

"I need more time, Superman," Batman said calmly.

Nodding, Superman struggled to fly back into battle.

Cyzarro and Batzarro impatiently watched Batman and Cyborg working on the ship.

"I can break for you," Cyzarro offered.

Cyborg shook his head. "That's what we're worried about."

Batzarro grunted in frustration, then shoved Cyborg and Batman out of the way. "Cyzarro, break now!"

Cyzarro hurtled over Cyborg, and punched his arm into the ship's console. A wave of electricity shot up his arm, blasting everyone off their feet.

But the ship's engine began to hum.

"He fixed it," Batman said, amazed.

"Of course," Cyborg realized. "Only a Bizarro can make technology work here."

Batman hopped in the cockpit, piloting the ship toward the destroyer.

Meanwhile, Superman redoubled his attacks against Darkseid, punching the villain repeatedly to little effect. Darkseid grabbed Superman again and hurled him against a wall atop the destroyer. "*Oof*," said Superman. "Not fun."

"You're too late, Superman," said Darkseid. "I now have enough of this bizarre energy to rule the galaxy."

Superman groaned, stumbling back onto his feet. "Well," he said bravely, "on Bizarro world, rules are meant to be broken."

Darkseid turned around.

Batman hovered behind him in his new ship, ready to fire.

OOF.

BOOM!

"Bizarro save day!" screamed Bizarro, jumping in front of Batman's ship. He hurled Lex Luthor's cylindrical bomb at Darkseid.

It exploded in a blast of bright-green energy.

Superman yelled as he fell off the destroyer, tumbling down on the rocks below.

Batman's ship exploded into pieces. Luckily, he was able to eject in time.

But Darkseid was unhurt. He smiled at Bizarro. "A Kryptonite bomb," he said. "Thank you." He lowered himself down into his destroyer and sat on his throne.

"Desaad," said Darkseid, "let us test our weapon on Earth."

CHAPTER 9: BIZARRO: ZERO OR HERO?

DESAAD PRESSED A BUTTON.

A cannon poked out of the top of the destroyer, and fired a massive beam of power.

It zapped the moon, transforming it into a cube.

Then the beam whizzed toward Earth.

Suddenly, a ship soared soared into the ray's path. It was Hawkman! "Hawk jet, inbound!" he shouted. "Deploying hawk swords! Pressing hawk button!"

A multitude of giant glowing swords swirled around the jet, forming a vast bird of purple energy that blocked the beam.

"Hawkman," Batman called over the radio, "did you manage to intercept the ray?"

Hawkman's jet shook so badly it felt like it might explode. "You could say that."

Back on Bizarro World, the Justice and Bizarro Leagues gathered around the fallen Superman.

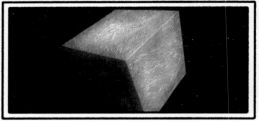

"Hawkman is holding off the ray," Batman reported to the group, "but I suspect his armor will eventually fall to the weirdiation."

"Bizarro tried to help," sobbed Bizarro.

"Yeah, you helped, all right!" Green Lantern yelled. "You helped Darkseid! Thanks to you, Earth is toast! Without Superman, we can't stop him."

"Yes," moaned Superman. "Yes, you can."

Everyone moved closer to hear Superman's weak voice.

"Darkseid's ship is somehow being protected

from the weirdiation," whispered Superman, "but if we overload the ship with those crazy rocks . . ."

Batman threw up his hands. "But that'll just make his weapon stronger," he said. "So this is how you destroy us all!"

Superman met Batman's eyes. "You need to trust me."

"Trust you?" said Batman. He turned away, biting his lip, squeezing his hands to fists.

Finally, Batman let out a long breath. "Well . . ." he said, "if there's one place I can try trusting you, it's on a backward world."

Bizarro pointed to the crystals. "No!" he cried. "Those are Bizarro's people! His friends."

WE CAN'T STOP HIM!

"I know, Bizarro," said Superman. He waved his hand at the other Bizarros. "But you have new friends now . . . and an old one, too."

Bizarro's mouth dropped open. "Superman Bizarro's friend?"

"Not just friends, Bizarro," Superman said sincerely. "*Brothers*. I should have been a better one to you."

Bizarro grinned. "Twin brothers?"

Superman nodded. "Fraternal, but yes. Twins."

Bizarro grunted happily. Then he marched into his city and tossed his crystal citizens into the hopper of Darkseid's destroyer.

"Good-bye," sobbed Bizarro. "Bizarro miss you."

Greenzarro, Bizarra, Batzarro, and Cyzarro joined Bizarro in throwing citizens into the destroyer's hopper. The Justice League helped, too.

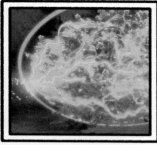

"I miss you!" Bizarro told another crystal citizen before hurling him up into the enormous pile. Bolts of electricity shot through the hopper, crossing over into the ship as the crystals overloaded the systems.

Fireballs exploded along the destroyer's sides.

A huge blast launched the head-shaped cockpit into deep space, hurtling Darkseid far away from Bizarro World.

Across the galaxy, Hawkman had nearly lost his struggle to keep the beam from reaching Earth. "Must keep pressing button! So hard!"

Then the ray fizzled out.

Hawkman started to celebrate . . . but the moon was still a cube.

On Bizarro World, the Justice League and Bizarro League waited for Batzarro to examine Superman.

"Superman A-OK," announced Batzarro.

"That's great," said Cyborg. "He's going to be all right, then?"

"No," replied Batman. "Batzarro means we can't save him."

Wonder Woman lowered her head. "Good-bye, Kal," she whispered.

Bizarro stood next to Superman. "Superman live."

"Stop with the opposite talk, man!" cried Cyborg.

Bizarro shook his head. "No. Superman live!" He

sucked in a deep breath, inhaling the glowing Kryptonite radiation from the Man of Steel. As Superman's complete opposite, Kryptonite was totally harmless to him. Bizarro let out a big burp.

Superman raised his head. "You . . ." he muttered, "saved the day, Bizarro."

Bizarro grinned as his friends slapped him on the back. "Bad job!" cheered Batzarro.

Batman kneeled beside Superman. "I'm not wrong often," he admitted, "but I was about you. You can be trusted."

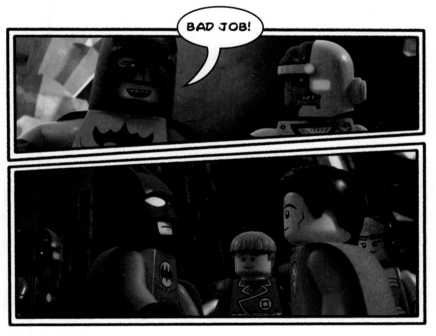

"Really?" Superman asked. "Then I guess you won't need that box of Kryptonite anymore."

"Let's not go crazy," said Batman.

Superman climbed shakily to his feet. "Well, if we're going to have a wildcard on the team who keeps tabs on me, I'm glad it's you," he told Batman. He stared at the wrecked landscape. "*Whoa*, look at this place."

Bizarro heaved a big sigh. "Bizarro lost whole world."

"Then we're going to have to rebuild it together," declared Superman.

Both the Bizarro League and the Justice League put their combined efforts into rebuilding the strange civilization on Bizarro World.

"Great job!" said Superman, looking around at the crystal construction. "In fact, the whole place looks wonderful. I can't wait to walk through that front door."

"*Hmm*," said Bizarro. "Front door."

THE END

SCHOLASTIC INC.

ADAPTED BY J. E. BRIGHT

SCRIPT WRITTEN BY JIM KRIEG

ATTACK OF THE
LEGION OF DOOM!

ISBN 978-1-338-03524-7

10 9 8 7 6 5 4 3 2 1   16 17 18 19 20

Printed in the U.S.A.   40

This edition first printing 2016

Book design by Erin McMahon

CHAPTER 1: A NEW LEADER

ON A DARK STREET IN METROPOLIS, the intergalactic villain Darkseid stood triumphantly on a hunk of rubble. Superman, Wonder Woman, Green Lantern, Hawkman, and The Flash lay on the ground, unconscious. Batman kneeled before Darkseid.

"And so the Justice League falls!" the criminal crowed. His eyes glowed, shooting deadly beams at Batman.

Cyborg leaped in front of Batman, blocking Darkseid's attack with an energy shield. The villain's beams ricocheted, blasting a wall. Bricks toppled on Darkseid.

THOOOM!

"Booyah!" Cyborg cheered. "Surrender now, Dorkseid!" He threw up his arms. "World's Best Cyborg!" he hollered. "Disco time!" As a glittering disco ball appeared overhead, the Justice League jumped to their feet and danced.

"I put the boogie in borg!" yelled Cyborg as he wiggled to the music.

Batman patted Cyborg's shoulder. "You saved my life," he said. "Impressive. We should hang out more. I've got a pool table back at the Batcave—"
R-R-R-RING!

Cyborg woke up. He was suspended in his charging station in the Hall of Justice. "*Ah*, dang.

I overslept!" he cried. "I'm going to be late for the meeting . . . again!" Cyborg scrambled out of his room, ran through the corridors of the Hall of Justice, and skidded into the Great Room. Superman, Batman, Wonder Woman, The Flash, and Green Lantern watched him enter.

"You're late, Cyborg," growled Batman.

"*Uh*, hi, everybody," Cyborg said sheepishly as he took a seat.

"Vic," asked Green Lantern, "don't you have an atomic clock built into you?"

"Think nothing of it, young Cyborg," Superman interrupted. "We started without you."

Superman raised his hand for attention. "It's Election Day," he said. "We'll be voting for a new hero to lead the Justice League." Behind Superman, holograms of his campaign posters appeared. "Please, everyone, vote with your heart."

The teammates pressed buttons on their consoles to vote. Batman peered up at the holographic display showing the results. "It looks like a tie, since Superman and I undoubtedly voted for ourselves."

Superman's eyes widened. "That never occurred to me," he said. "I voted for you."

"And the winner is . . . Batman!" announced Cyborg. "All right, Dark Knight!" He raised his palm for a high five, which Batman ignored.

The Trouble Alert flashed, clanging its alarm. The Justice League rushed over to the monitors.

"A robbery at the Metropolis First National Bank," said Wonder Woman.

The Flash tilted his head at Batman. "What's the word, chief?"

"The word," replied Batman, "is go."

The Justice League raced into their high-tech ship, the *Javelin*, and soared toward downtown Metropolis. As they arrived, a villain in a yellow outfit burst out of the bank's front doors to find the police waiting for him. The criminal giggled.

"Freeze!" a cop hollered. "Hold it right there, Joker!"

"I'm not the Joker!" the villain shouted back. "I'm the Trickster. Totally different."

Superman called, "Ah, our old friend, the Trickster."

"Finally!" replied the Trickster. "He gets me."

Superman leaned close in to his teammates so they could hear him whisper. "I know he isn't really our friend. I was being ironic." Then he flew between the villain and the police. "Come quietly, Trickster!"

The Trickster held up a canister. "You either let me go," he threatened, "or we're going to have a smelly situation on our hands."

"I got this!" shouted Cyborg. He shot a sonic blast at the Trickster, which spun the canister into the air. "And now to dispose of it." He took aim.

"Wait!" warned Batman. Cyborg fired his laser cannon. The canister exploded, releasing a noxious green gas, which drifted into the city.

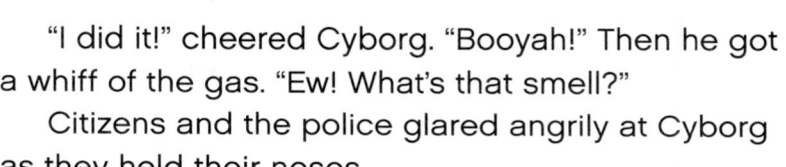

"I did it!" cheered Cyborg. "Booyah!" Then he got a whiff of the gas. "Ew! What's that smell?"

Citizens and the police glared angrily at Cyborg as they held their noses.

"Glad I'm not in his shoes," said Green Lantern. He created a giant fan with his power ring, and blew away some of the stinky gas.

"I was trying to tell you, Cyborg," Batman said, "that was a stink bomb. Now this whole section of the city stinks."

"Not to mention you guys," added The Flash.

The Trickster giggled as Superman dragged him off to jail. "Looks like I got the last laugh!"

Cyborg squirmed and said, "Oops?"

CHAPTER 2: AMBUSH AT AREA 52

CYBORG TRIED to get his mind off his embarrassment with what happened with the Trickster by tinkering with the technology of the Hall of Justice. He twisted a glowing bolt with a wrench. Electricity shot up his arm and sizzled his circuits. Cyborg fell backward, twitching.

BBZZZZZZAACK!

A robot he had built peered down at him worriedly. "Have Cyborg's functions terminated?"

"No, Cy-bot," groaned Cyborg, "I was working on some new upgrades for the Hall. I'm distracted. I made a big, stinky mess today, and I'm not so sure the others want me around."

With a sigh, Cyborg climbed to his feet. He strode out of the equipment room. Cyborg walked to the Great Hall, where he found his teammates. *"Whoa!"* he gasped. "What's going on?"

"Our former costumes were ruined with a permanent stench," Batman answered. "It compromised our effectiveness as crime fighters."

Cyborg looked down at his boots. "Right," he whispered, "because it's my fault your old ones got all stinky."

"Nonsense," said Wonder Woman. "We all needed a change. Why don't we come up with something new for you, too?"

"We can't," replied Batman. "Cyborg doesn't wear clothes."

A loud alarm echoed in the Great Hall and red lights flashed.

"The Trouble Alert!" announced Superman. An angry military man with a white moustache appeared on screen.

"Justice League," the man said, "I am General Lane, commanding officer of Area 52, a top-secret government installation. We are under attack from person or persons unknown. But it's probably . . . alien."

"You say that like it's a bad thing, general," replied Superman.

"Just get over here," insisted General Lane, "and take—"

The image fuzzed out in snowy static. "Let's go," said The Flash. "I can feel myself growing older just standing here."

Superman put his hand on The Flash's shoulder. "Not so fast. Batman is our elected leader. This is his call."

The members of the Justice League waited for Batman's decision.

"Prepare the *Javelin* for launch," said Batman.

In their supersonic craft, the Justice League soared toward Area 52. "Look alive, team," ordered Batman as the *Javelin* began to descend. "We've entered Area 52 airspace."

"Ooh," said Cyborg, "a spooky, top-secret government compound. How'd you even know where to find it?"

Batman narrowed his eyes. "I'm—"

"Batman," Cyborg finished. "Right. Gotcha."

The *Javelin* landed on the tarmac of Area 52. The Justice League stepped out into the eerie silent stillness of the base.

"It's quiet," said Batman. "Too quiet."

"Truck!" screamed Cyborg. He pointed up at the sky, where a huge sixteen-wheeler big rig tumbled toward them.

Green Lantern created a force-field dome that saved the team from getting crushed. When the dust cleared, the Justice League was amazed to see a group of super-villains standing on the tarmac. Captain Cold, Gorilla Grodd, Cheetah, and Black Manta struck a dramatic pose.

Hovering above them was Sinestro. "Welcome to your defeat, Justice League," he said, creating giant yellow words behind him with his power ring. "Defeat at the hands of . . . the Legion of Doom!"

"Copyright and trademark," added Captain Cold.

CHAPTER 3: BATTLE ON THE BASE

"DESTROY THEM," Sinestro ordered the Legion of Doom.

"Justice League, move out," commanded Batman."

"You heard our captain," cried Superman, swooping into the air. "Let's move!"

While Green Lantern battled Captain Cold, Cheetah pounced at Wonder Woman. "The Legion of Doom will have your heads!" Cheetah screeched.

Wonder Woman sidestepped, and grabbed Cheetah's tail. "Tails, you lose," said Wonder Woman. She spun Cheetah around in a circle.

Nearby, Gorilla Grodd bounded toward Superman. Before he got close, Superman exhaled sharply, blowing the muscular ape through the wall of an airplane hangar.

Superman flew in the hole, scanning the inside of the dark warehouse. "It's no use trying to hide from me!"

"Who's hiding?" growled Grodd. Brilliant lights flashed as Grodd rose up atop a spinning flying saucer. "I'm just getting a feel for my new ride." He shot energy rays at Superman, nailing him in the chest.

"Hey!" cried Superman. "I felt that!" He dodged around the rays, zooming through the hangar.

Outside, Sinestro flew above Cyborg, who ran across the tarmac. "School's in session, youngster," yelled Sinestro, trying to hit Cyborg with a giant yellow sledgehammer.

Cyborg shot his arm cannons at Sinestro as he ran. "Well, here's my homework!"

Sinestro avoided Cyborg's attack, and took careful aim. He blasted Cyborg with an energy beam, knocking him into a pile of crates. "Class dismissed."

"Hey, Sinestro!" The Flash hollered behind him, racing closer at super-speed. "Here comes your worst nightmare."

"My worst nightmare involves public speaking in my underwear," replied Sinestro. "You're not even close." He created a speeding train and aimed it at The Flash.

The Flash rushed along the side of the train, zipping toward Sinestro. "All aboard the haymaker express," he exclaimed as he hit Sinestro hard. "Ha, ticket punched!"

Sinestro spun around, dizzy, but he cleared his head quickly. "Take this, you parasitic pinball," he sneered, creating bumpers and paddles around The Flash.

The Flash got caught in the pinball game, bouncing around. "Whoa!" he cried, falling down.

"Full tilt, loser," said Sinestro. He lowered himself to where Cyborg was alone. "Now to finish off the half-man." He created another gigantic hammer to smash Cyborg.

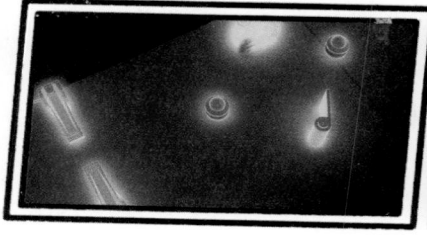

Cyborg protected himself under a small energy dome. With every smash of Sinestro's hammer, the dome held, but the ground around it cracked.

"So, robot man," Sinestro teased, "is that all you can do? Sit there while the real men do the work?"

As Batman and Black Manta battled nearby, Wonder Woman stopped spinning Cheetah and let her go. Cheetah tumbled through the air, and grabbed ahold of Gorilla Grodd's head as he passed by on his flying saucer. She clung to his face.

"You frustrating feline," gasped Grodd. "I can't see!" The saucer tilted and dipped.

Taking advantage of Grodd's distraction, Superman landed on the edge of the UFO, running on it to make it spin wildly.

The saucer whizzed out of control, smashing to the ground. Grodd and Cheetah skidded across the tarmac and ended up in a heap.

With a sonic boom, Lex Luthor appeared in a cosmic tunnel next to them. He had a big cylindrical container with him. "Legion of Doom!" Lex called. "Mission accomplished. Let us make our victorious retreat!"

CHAPTER 4: STOLEN ALIEN

"WHAT'S LEX GOT THERE?" asked Superman.

" Nothing good," replied Batman.

The inter-dimensional tunnel retracted and vanished, taking Lex Luthor and the cylinder with it.

Having heard Lex's call to retreat, Sinestro started to fly away, but Cyborg fired a grappling hook and caught the villain's ankle. Sinestro created a buzz saw and cut Cyborg's cord. Then he turned the saw into a gigantic dustpan. "Here's a pop quiz," he told Cyborg, swatting him with the pan. "You failed."

Sinestro swooped over the tarmac, scooping up his fallen teammates with the dustpan. "Once again, it's up to me to clean up after lesser people's messes." He carried the other members of the Legion of Doom over to Black Manta's ship.

Superman soared after them, but before he could grab the ship, it launched, vanishing at warp speed.

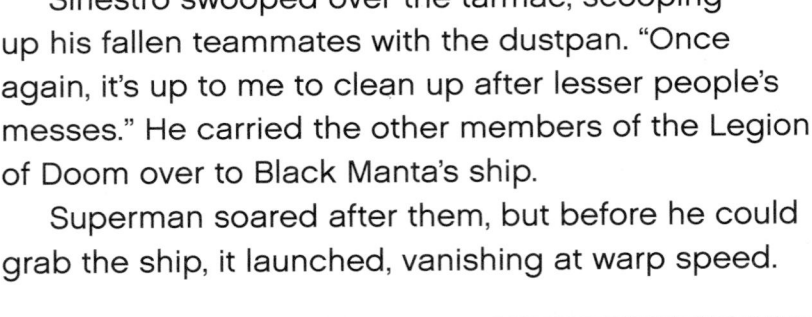

General Lane stormed over to the group. "You let them get away!"

"So, what? The only thing they got was a giant can of soda or something," said Green Lantern.

The general held up a file with a picture of the cylinder on the front. "It was an alien!" he yelled. "And you let it slip through your fingers because of your incompetence." He narrowed his eyes at Superman. "How do I know all you aliens aren't in cahoots?"

"Hey!" argued The Flash. "Superman isn't an alien! He's a . . . oh, yeah, I guess he kind of is."

Superman hovered above General Lane. "The real question is," he said, "why are you incarcerating aliens?"

"*Ah*, well . . . " stammered the general. "I'm not the one being questioned here! Now, if you'll excuse me, I've got government property to locate." General Lane strode away.

Superman looked worried. "Surely our government isn't arresting extraterrestrials."

"Based on my analysis of his behavior," replied Batman, "it's more likely that General Lane has greatly exceeded his authority."

Cyborg hung his head, looking sad.

"Why the long face, Cyborg?" asked Superman. "You held your own against a formidable opponent. Good job!"

"Good job?" cried Cyborg. "If it wasn't for me we could have stopped them."

"You're still the youngest member of this team," Wonder Woman said gently. "Cut yourself some slack."

"The question is," said Batman, "what happens next time we meet?"

CHAPTER 5: MELTDOWN

IN THE BASEMENT of the Hall of Justice, Cyborg and Cy-bot added cables and specialized bricks to the technology of the headquarters. Cyborg touched the wrong circuit. Bolts of energy zapped him and Cy-bot. They fell onto their backs. "It's no use," said Cyborg, sitting up. "Not even my hobby can clear my mind. I need some advice."

"Can't get up," moaned Cy-bot. "Help."

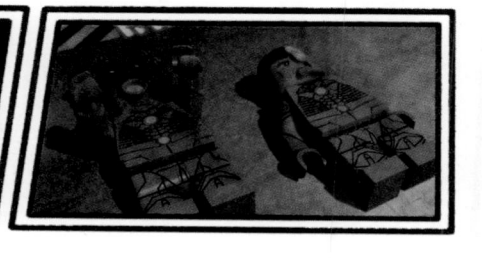

Cyborg strode out of the basement. He found Wonder Woman on the roof watching the sunset.

"Listen, Vic," said Wonder Woman, "you look at your recent battles and see mistakes. That's just your perception, but it's certainly not my perception

of you." Cyborg smiled slightly. "You're a young hero," Wonder Woman continued. "You have to trust your instincts and give yourself time to grow."

Cyborg nodded. "So," he said, "you're saying I should really beef up my cybernetic components?"

"What?" blurted Wonder Woman. "No."

"Thanks, Wonder Woman!" cheered Cyborg. "That's exactly what I'll do!" He rushed off the roof. Moments later, he was welding in his workshop.

WHAT'S UP?

"I don't know why I didn't think of it before," he said as he attached an enormous cannon onto his shoulder with Cy-bot's help. "I've got to gear up! Booyah!"

With an array of new weapons, Cyborg strolled confidently through the corridors. He passed Batman on the way to the Great Hall. "What's up?" he asked.

Batman ignored him.

A few seconds later, Cyborg strode past Green Lantern. "How's it going, Hal?"

"I'm living the dream, Vic," Green Lantern replied.

Cyborg resumed walking toward the Great Hall.

Then he passed Batman again. "Batman," he said with a nod.

"Have a nice day," said Batman, walking on.

Cyborg whistled as he strolled. He stopped, and rushed back toward Batman. "This may sound strange," said Cyborg, "but I passed you twice, and I don't think—"

Batman glared. "Perhaps if you concentrated on being a super hero instead of butting into other people's business, you'd be a better Justice League member."

With a gulp, Cyborg backed off. "Sorry," he said, his feelings hurt. He hurried away. When Cyborg reached the Great Hall, Superman, Wonder Woman, and Batman were entering at the same time.

Cyborg gathered his courage and approached Batman. "Hey," he said, "maybe that was meant to be constructive criticism when I passed you just now, but—"

"I didn't say anything when you walked by," replied Batman. "You must be getting a double image in your cybernetic eye. Let me help." He smacked the side of Cyborg's head, causing his eyes to spin. "There," said Batman. "Better?"

The red lights and sirens of the Trouble Alert blared.

Cyborg rushed over the monitor. "It's that prototype Nuketron Reactor that just went online," he said. "The one that should provide a solution to the world's energy needs."

"By Hippolyta's hairnet," swore Wonder Woman. "It's in danger of a total meltdown."

"Let's go," said Batman.

The Justice League flew in the *Javelin* toward the Nuketron Reactor. As they got close, the heroes looked out the window at the building below. It was a giant dome in the center of the city. Red lights flashed around it as steam rose from cracks in the dome.

"Cyborg," asked Green Lantern, "how long before the energy core melts down?"

Cyborg peered down through his cybernetic eye. "This is strange," he reported. "My readouts don't detect anything wrong. Everything looks normal."

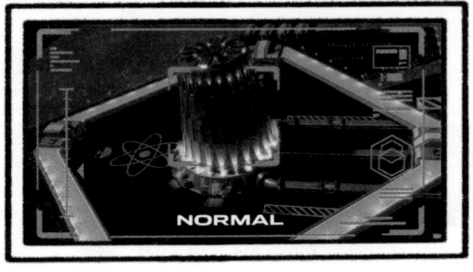

"Time for an oil change, Tin Man?" Green Lantern asked. "Look at that thing. That's about as normal as Batman smiling."

Batman faced his team. "Cyborg and I will secure the perimeter," he instructed. "Flash, you and Wonder Woman get the crew out of that inferno. Superman and Hal, you're both immune to the reactor's radiation. Stop the energy core from melting down . . . or else Metropolis becomes a lifeless radiation hot zone for the next 10,000 years."

"*Uh*, that's a pep talk?" asked Green Lantern.

"Let's do this, guys!" The Flash whizzed across the lot where workmen used a crane to hoist bricks. He zoomed in and grabbed them. "Don't worry, fellas! I'll have you out of danger in a flash!"

Cyborg and Batman hurried toward the plant. Cyborg blinked his robotic eye. "Batman," he warned, "I'm still reading everything is normal."

"We'll deal with your software glitches when we get back to the Hall," said Batman.

CHAPTER 6: CAMERA ONE/ CAMERA TWO

AS HE AND CYBORG reached the reactor, Batman activated his comlink. "Superman, Hal," he asked, "what do you see?"

On the other side of the site, Green Lantern soared above a damaged pipeline. "The coolant pump between the water supply and reactor core is toast," he reported. "No wonder it's overheating."

Superman swooped over the reactor's dome and scanned it with his X-ray vision. Inside, he saw a woman holding a video camera in the control room. It was Lois Lane! A violent rumble shook the reactor. A heavy piece of computer equipment fell off the wall, pinning Lois underneath. Superman blasted through the reactor wall, smashing his way through the building's layers.

Superman grabbed the equipment and tossed it aside. "There you go, Lois." Sirens blared, and Superman scanned the damaged core. Its coolant had dropped to dangerous levels. "Now let's get you out of here before—"

To Superman's surprise, she had vanished entirely. "Lois?"

An explosion rocked the reactor. Superman was blasted against a wall as the room glowed red-hot. He winced at the intense radioactive heat. "Batman," he reported, "the core temperature is hotter than the sun. We're in full meltdown!"

"You have to cool the core to a safer temperature long enough to get it out of the building," replied Batman.

"I'll do my best," said Superman. He inhaled deeply, then released his freeze breath.

Ice rippled over the core's sizzling surface. It cooled the core a little . . . but not enough to keep it from melting down.

Superman charged underneath the shielded core, and heaved it up on his shoulders. Together, he and Green Lantern pushed the core out through the top of the reactor, shoving it upward until they had left the Earth's atmosphere.

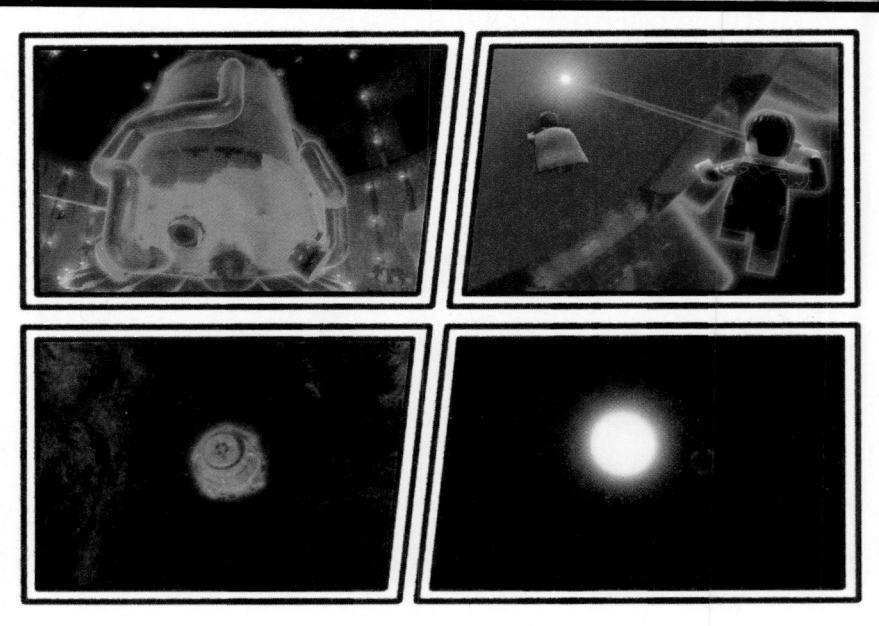

Up at the edge of outer space, Superman gathered his strength. "Hold steady and get ready," he told Green Lantern. "Here . . . we . . . go!" Superman hurled the core away from the Earth. The core exploded halfway to the sun.

"Saved the day," said Green Lantern. "Again!" He and Superman smiled at one another, and they headed back to Metropolis.

Down in the reactor, Cyborg reached the room where the core had been. He stared at the mess, first with his human eye. He saw the melted room that Superman and Green Lantern had dismantled. "Camera one," said Cyborg.

Then Cyborg looked at the room with his robotic eye. "Camera two," he said. The only damage was from Superman's freeze breath and Green Lantern's ring. He looked at Batman. "Something's funny here," he explained. "And I mean funny messed up, not funny ha-ha. There was never anything wrong with the reactor."

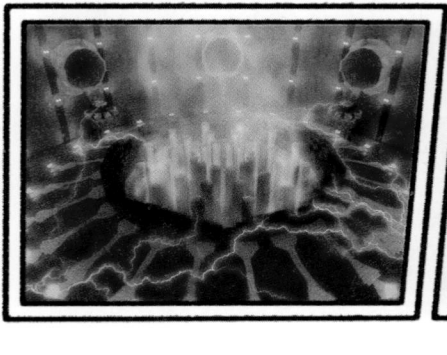 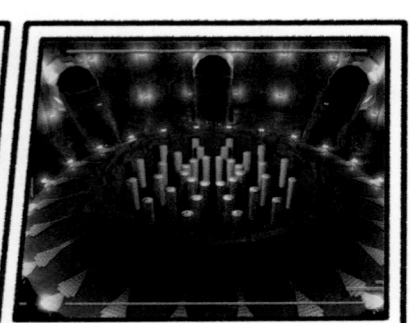

The Justice League gathered around Cyborg and Batman as Green Lantern and Superman returned to Earth. "I'm beginning to think you're right," said Batman, although he was facing in the other direction, staring at a large crowd of reporters, police officers and angry plant workers.

"Why did you destroy our power plant?" one man demanded.

Superman cleared his throat. "You may not have noticed your plant was experiencing. . ." He trailed

off as he saw that the reactor looked completely different. "A meltdown?"

"Now it looks less melty," said The Flash.

Lois Lane rushed up to Superman with her camera. "You and the League have just destroyed a multibillion dollar power plant that could have made Metropolis a world leader in efficient energy production," she said. "What do you have to say for yourselves?"

"Lois?" exclaimed Superman. "You're okay."

"Okay?" shouted Lois. "I'm livid, like everyone else on Earth. What do you tell your critics who claim the Justice League has too much power?"

"*Whoa*," said Green Lantern. "What critics?"

"My daddy, for one," replied Lois.

General Lane stepped up beside Lois with a stern expression.

"He's your daddy?" Wonder Woman asked.

Cyborg scratched his head. "Who's your daddy?"

"I knew he was your daddy," said Batman.

"There was no meltdown," declared General Lane. "The reactor was working fine." He faced the crowd. "Do you see, people? We let superpowered goons run around unrestricted and this is the type of thing that is bound to happen. The so-called Justice League needs to pay for its crimes," the general continued. "They must be controlled before something worse takes their place."

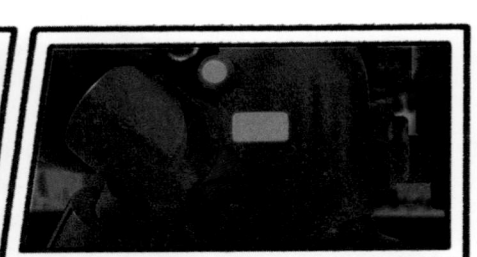

"Down with the Justice League!" a workman yelled.

An angry woman added, "I used to like them but now I don't!"

Cyborg covered his human eye and peered at the mob. In the back was a green alien! He gasped and lowered his hand. The alien vanished.

"People, people," Superman said. "Don't panic. This has apparently been one big misunderstanding. The Justice League is all about responsibility. I'm sure that once we've explained everything, the World Court will happily find us—"

CHAPTER 7: BANISHED

"GUILTY AS CHARGED! For the charges of stink bombing Metropolis, attacking a government facility, and nearly causing a nuclear meltdown," General Lane read from the verdict, "the Justice League is banished from Planet Earth! Effective immediately!"

"All right," growled Batman, "this conspiracy has gone far enough. We have to get to the bottom of it." He started to slink offstage. "We're going dark. Off the grid. We'll work from the shadows to solve this mystery—"

"Nope," said Superman, grabbing Batman by his cape. "Not this time. The Justice League was formed to serve the governments of the world. They overrule your authority, Batman. If they want us gone, we go."

"Nice speech, alien," said General Lane. "Guards, get these heroes out of my sight."

Later that afternoon, the members of the Justice League packed up their belongings and loaded them into the *Javelin*. Then they launched out of the Hall of Justice roof, heading into outer space, leaving Earth behind.

Green Lantern sat next to Cyborg in the ship. Cyborg trembled robotically as they passed the moon. "Wipe away those tears, Cyborg," said Green Lantern. "It's a big galaxy. Stick with me and we'll have a blast. I know a planet inhabited by broken toasters. Maybe we'll find you a girlfriend."

Wonder Woman joined Superman in the cockpit. "I think you can let go of Batman now."

"Oh," said Superman, releasing him. "Sorry about that. But the law is the law."

Batman smoothed down his uniform. "We'll discuss your little mutiny later. Our job now is to gather evidence, prove we were framed, and then return to Earth."

"I'm afraid returning to Earth is not an option," sneered Sinestro.

The Justice League glanced up to see the yellow villain floating in space.

"I just came to give you a farewell gift," said Sinestro.

"I hope you kept the receipt," Green Lantern retorted.

The *Javelin* fired its weapons, but Sinestro created a yellow energy shield. He yawned as the beams bounced away.

"Keep firing!" insisted Green Lantern. "He'll have to keep up that shield and won't be able to attack."

"Think so?" asked Sinestro. He held up a tablet. "Meet my new best friend. It's called a Father Box."

He activated it, creating a huge, swirling tunnel disappearing into space. "Doesn't this just bowl you over? Prepare to be flushed to the other side of the galaxy!" Then Sinestro created a humongous plunger, and shoved the *Javelin* into the cosmic tube.

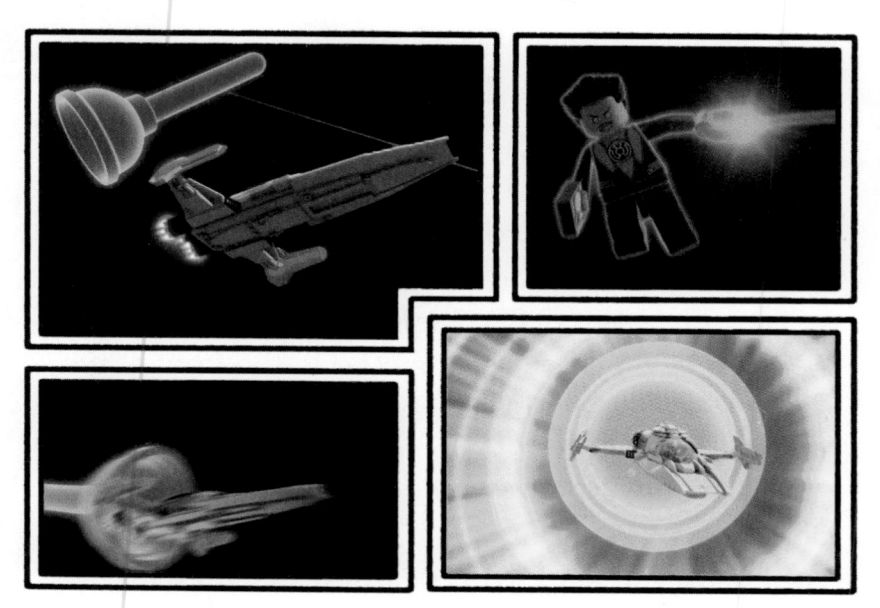

With a whooshing sound, the *Javelin* swirled through the portal.

"Oh, I get it," said The Flash. "Bowl! Flush! Like a toilet."

Then he and the Justice League screamed as they spun into another dimension.

CHAPTER 8: MARTIAN MIND CONTROL

THE JAVELIN SPAT OUT of the tunnel in the farthest reaches of the galaxy, beside a vast black hole. "We're caught in the pull!" Green Lantern yelled. "Everybody hang tight!"

Green Lantern exited the *Javelin*, and created a small spaceship around himself. His ship launched a strong tether, which connected to the front of the *Javelin*. The line snapped taut as Green Lantern tried to tow the Justice League to safety.

HANG TIGHT!

"I'm giving her all the willpower I've got, but I can't escape the black hole's gravity," Green Lantern reported. "At least we're not being sucked in anymore. You guys all right back there?"

"S'all right," muttered Cyborg. He fizzled with electricity and fell to pieces. Chunks of him slammed into the back wall.

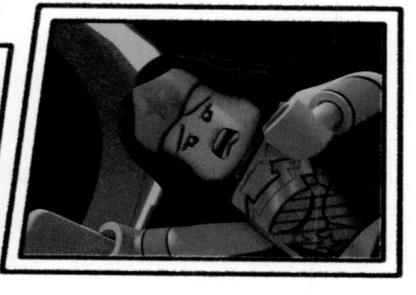

"Oh, poor friend," gasped Wonder Woman. "I shall sing the Themysciran Song of Dead Heroes for you!"

Batman held up his hand. "No need to sing. He's just a dummy."

"That doesn't matter," said Superman. "He was our friend!"

The Flash picked up Cyborg's head. "No, he means a real dummy," he explained, showing the team that the head actually belonged to Cy-bot. "He was acting weird ever since takeoff."

"Which leaves us with two questions," said

Batman. "How do we get out of this jam . . . and where is the real Cyborg?"

The real Cyborg was in the Hall of Justice. He was adjusting the electronics in a wall panel. "I hate to leave the guys in the lurch," he muttered, "but I know there is something fishy going on." He shook a monitor, and a strange device dropped onto the floor.

"A clue," said Cyborg, picking it up. "Some kind of weird alien technology. How'd this get here? Better check the security tapes."

Cyborg fast-forwarded through the camera footage, and spotted a strange alien wandering the halls. "Oh, I know you," he said. He checked his own camera's footage from the power plant.

"Aha!" crowed Cyborg. "That's the alien I saw. I knew he couldn't be some random green guy in red underwear. Now all I have to do is get this evidence out there and clear the Justice League."

"Clear them with whom?" asked Sinestro.

Cyborg whirled around to see the yellow villain floating in the Great Hall.

"Within a few hours," Sinestro said, "the Legion of Doom will have taken over the world. Only one member of the Justice League left . . . and it's the weakest one." He laughed. "I think you already know how this ends, don't you, half-man?"

Cyborg shot a sonic blast above Sinestro's head.

"You missed," said Sinestro.

Then a chunk of blasted ceiling toppled down on Sinestro, flattening him.

Cyborg rushed outside. "Got to keep moving," he gasped. "This evidence is more important than me getting payback."

"Go ahead, run!" shouted Sinestro. "It'll make your final defeat more enjoyable."

Cyborg leaped away from Sinestro's fire. He bounced across the gardens, and clambered up the side of the building to the roof.

Sinestro cornered him, but before he could deal a wallop, he stopped and looked worried. "What?" the villain gasped. "The Justice League? Alive! Impossible." He glared maniacally at invisible people around him.

The green alien materialized behind him. "Not impossible," he said, placing his hand on Sinestro's head, "for me."

Sinestro's eyes blanked out. "You are under my mental control," the alien said. The alien lowered him down to Cyborg.

"You're the shape-shifter who set us up," said Cyborg. "What did you do to him?"

"Martians like me have the ability to influence minds," the alien explained. "Organic minds. Unlike yours, Cyborg."

Cyborg nodded. "Everyone else saw the plant malfunctioning because you were making them see that," he realized. "But my cyber-organic brain is immune to your powers." Cyborg pointed his sonic cannon at the Martian. "I still don't trust you."

"Please," the alien said. "I am here to help."

"Like you helped the heroes of Earth get banished?" argued Cyborg.

The Martian hung his head. "I was tricked. Lex Luthor freed me. I let my thirst for vengeance cloud my judgment. Forgive me. Let me make this right."

"How?" Cyborg asked.

Again, the Martian placed his hand on Sinestro's head. Sinestro raised his power ring and activated the Father Box that created a galactic tunnel.

"All right, Sinestro," said the alien. "It's time to unflush the Justice League."

Sinestro laughed. "Flush. That's a good one."
The tunnel circled into another dimension.

In front of the black hole, Batman, in his spacesuit, pushed against a wing of the *Javelin*. Superman pushed on the other wing, while Wonder Woman heaved against the tail fin. In front, Green Lantern's ship pulled on the tether. The Flash sat inside, working the controls in the cockpit.

"Keep pushing!" Green Lantern insisted.

"The *Javelin* is a state-of-the-art spacecraft," Batman grumbled. "I never thought we'd have to

get out and push." His eyes widened as a portal
appeared in front of Green Lantern's ship.

"Athena's fallen arches!" shouted Wonder Woman.
"Our way home! Everyone heave!"

Inch by inch, the *Javelin* shifted toward the
portal. Seconds after they made it through, the
tunnel swirled closed.

CHAPTER 9: DOOM IN METROPOLIS

BACK ON EARTH, the Justice League rushed into their headquarters. They saw on the monitors that the takeover of Metropolis by the Legion of Doom was already underway. The Hall of Doom floated over the city, raining down destruction on the buildings and citizens.

AAAAAH!

"Okay, here's the plan," said Batman. "Hal, you, The Flash, and Wonder Woman take out the Hall of Doom. Superman and I will stop Grodd and the forces on the ground."

"What about me?" asked Cyborg.

"I need you to stay in the Hall, Cyborg," replied Batman. "Hold down the fort, and also keep an eye on this Martian."

Cyborg bit his lip. "But I want to go with you."

Batman looked into Cyborg's eyes. "By going rogue, like I wanted to do, you saved us all. But now I need you to make sure Sinestro and the Martian stay put. Can you do that, soldier?"

Cyborg sighed. "Yes, sir."

A few minutes later, Grodd advanced along an avenue atop a tank as his mechanical monkeys rampaged. He pounded his chest. "Victory is ours!"

"Not quite," said Batman. The Dark Knight swung onto a ledge, armored in his Bat-Mech. "Don't worry, Grodd. You can have all the bananas you want in Blackgate Prison."

Gorilla Grodd pointed at Batman. "Destroy him!"

The tanks fired laser beams, but Superman swooped down, blocking them with his chest. The robot apes attacked, too, but in his suit, Batman handled them easily.

High above Metropolis, Green Lantern and Wonder Woman flew toward the sinister Hall of Doom.

Cheetah announced to Wonder Woman, "I've got a little surprise for you!" She fired laser beams.

Wonder Woman deflected the lasers with her silver bracelets.

"*Uh*," said Cheetah, "that wasn't the surprise. This is the surprise!" She launched tentacles out of the side of the Hall of Doom, which bound around Wonder Woman.

Wonder Woman flexed, bursting the tentacles apart.

"We're out of surprises," Cheetah told Lex Luthor inside. "How do we stop her?"

Lex Luthor made a fist. "By exploiting her one weakness," he answered "Her compassion! Launch missiles!" Two fiery missiles trailed out of the Hall of Doom, passing Wonder Woman on either side.

"You missed!" shouted Wonder Woman.

"Did I?" Lex replied.

Wonder Woman whirled around. The missiles hit the base of a skyscraper. The building teetered, and slowly fell toward an animal hospital.

"No!" screamed Wonder Woman. She zoomed toward the falling building at top speed. It had fallen

too far for her to push it upright—all she could do was hold it in place.

Down below, Superman hurled tanks, smashing them. "You're less fun than a barrel of monkeys!" he shouted.

A green beam shot from the Hall of Doom. It hit Superman square in the back.

Superman screamed and flattened against the street. "No! Kryptonite . . ." he gasped.

KRYPTONITE . . .

Batman had challenged Gorilla Grodd in hand-to-hand combat when he saw Superman was in trouble. "Hold on!" he hollered. "I'm coming!"

Another beam fired down from the Hall of Doom, blasting Batman's armor into smithereens.

Grodd grabbed Batman and hoisted him into the air, laughing victoriously.

In the Hall of Justice, Cyborg and the Martian gaped at the destruction on the monitors.

The Martian shook his head. "The Hall of Doom was specifically designed to withstand your powers and exploit your weaknesses. It is only a matter of time before it defeats the entire Justice League."

"Not the entire League," replied Cyborg. "I have an idea!"

CHAPTER 10: HALL AGAINST HALL

CYBORG RAN TO A CONTROL PANEL and plugged wires from his arm into the ports. Lights flashed and the Hall of Justice trembled.

The Martian struggled to keep his balance. "What's happening?"

"I gave it an upgrade," Cyborg said. "It's my hobby! Three . . . two . . . one . . . hold on!"

The Hall of Justice shuddered. Rockets underneath it ignited. It rose into the sky.

"Let's show them we've got style!" cheered Cyborg. "Launch disco missiles!"

Dozens of rockets with glittering disco-ball warheads shot out of the Hall of Justice.

The missiles smashed into the Hall of Doom and exploded.

Down on the street, Superman punched Gorilla Grodd so hard that he flew backward, crushing a tank. Batman fell free and Superman helped him up.

"Good to know you've got my back when it counts," said Batman.

Superman smiled at the destruction overhead. "Looks like Cyborg had all our backs."

"He's going to make a great leader someday," added Batman.

The two flying battle stations shot everything they had at one another. Even during the Hall of Doom's merciless final assault, Cyborg was prepared. "Star shield, activate!"

The Legion's attack bounced harmlessly off the Justice League's force field.

Cyborg grinned. "I call this my in-your-face finale," he told the Martian. Then he launched hundreds of missiles with a picture of him smiling on each one.

This final assault blasted the Hall of Doom. It fell, smoking and exploding, toward an empty park below. It smashed into the grass, digging up dirt and rocks, until it skidded to a stop.

The Hall of Justice landed next to the disabled Hall of Doom.

The Martian and Cyborg raced out of the headquarters. Cheetah, Black Manta, Captain Cold, and Lex Luthor had survived, and were limping away on foot.

"You aren't going anywhere!" yelled Cyborg. He took aim.

The Martian put his hand on Cyborg's arm. "Please," he said. "Leave this to me." He soared toward the villains, who attacked him with their remaining strength.

But the Martian knocked out Cheetah, Captain Cold, and Black Manta.

"Looks like you always get your man," said Cyborg. "Like you're a . . . Martian Manhunter!"

"*Hmm* . . . I like it," said Martian Manhunter.

Of the Legion of Doom, only Lex Luthor remained standing. He faced Martian Manhunter. "If it wasn't for me," Lex said, "you'd still be held prisoner."

"For that I am grateful," said Martian Manhunter.

Lex smiled. "So you'll let me go?"

"Yes," Martian Manhunter replied. "But they may not."

The Justice League surrounded him, glaring at Lex.

Later, as the Legion of Doom was loaded onto special police transports, a crowd of citizens gathered to celebrate. "Hooray, Justice League!" they shouted.

"Sorry we exiled you!" one man yelled. "Our bad!"

"Thanks to you, Cyborg, the Earth is out of danger because you trusted your instincts," said Batman. He held out his hand. "Good job."

Grinning, Cyborg shook Batman's hand.

Superman and Wonder Woman flanked Martian Manhunter. "I'm sorry about the way this planet treated you when you arrived," said Superman, "but sometimes we're suspicious of something we haven't seen before."

Batman looked at his watch. "According to the bylaws of the League, I'm only leader for another . . . 37 seconds. Then it'll be time for another election."

"You've still got my vote, Bats," said Superman.

Batman nodded at Martian Manhunter. "My final act as leader is to offer a Justice League membership to our new ally."

"In that case," said Superman, "welcome to the team, Martian Manhunter!"

Martian Manhunter bowed. "I not only have a new planet . . . but a new family."

The Justice League congratulated their new friend.

"Let's party!" Cyborg hollered.

"Not so fast!" said a gruff voice. General Lane strode over. "I'm holding you all responsible for this damage."

Superman winked at Martian Manhunter. The Martian's eyes glowed, and General Lane's eyes blanked out.

The general danced like a robot, and Cy-bot rushed over and boogied with him. The Justice League laughed and cheered.